T0417624

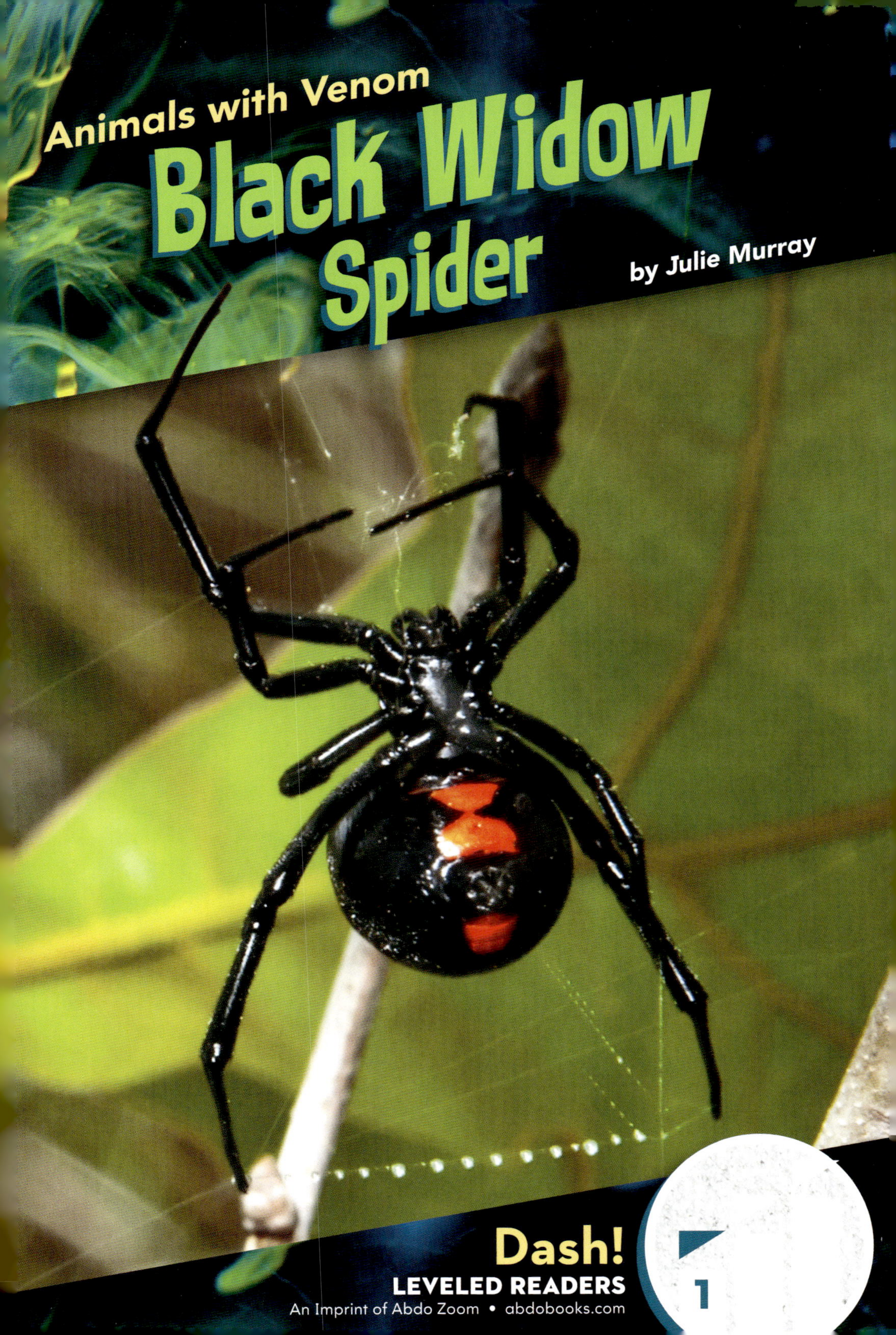
Animals with Venom
Black Widow Spider
by Julie Murray
Dash!
LEVELED READERS
An Imprint of Abdo Zoom • abdobooks.com
1

Level 1 – Beginning
Short and simple sentences with familiar words or patterns for children who are beginning to understand how letters and sounds go together.

Level 2 – Emerging
Longer words and sentences with more complex language patterns for readers who are practicing common words and letter sounds.

Level 3 – Transitional
More developed language and vocabulary for readers who are becoming more independent.

abdobooks.com

Published by Abdo Zoom, a division of ABDO, PO Box 398166, Minneapolis, Minnesota 55439.
Copyright © 2021 by Abdo Consulting Group, Inc. International copyrights reserved in all countries. No part of this book may be reproduced in any form without written permission from the publisher.
Dash!™ is a trademark and logo of Abdo Zoom.

Printed in the United States of America, North Mankato, Minnesota.
052020
092020

Photo Credits: Alamy, iStock, Minden Pictures, Shutterstock
Production Contributors: Kenny Abdo, Jennie Forsberg, Grace Hansen, John Hansen
Design Contributors: Dorothy Toth, Neil Klinepier, Candice Keimig

Library of Congress Control Number: 2019955551

Publisher's Cataloging in Publication Data

Names: Murray, Julie, author.
Title: Black widow spider / by Julie Murray
Description: Minneapolis, Minnesota : Abdo Zoom, 2021 | Series: Animals with venom | Includes online resources and index.
Identifiers: ISBN 9781098221010 (lib. bdg.) | ISBN 9781644943960 (pbk.) | ISBN 9781098221997 (ebook) | ISBN 9781098222482 (Read-to-Me ebook)
Subjects: LCSH: Black widow spider--Juvenile literature. | Hour-glass spider--Juvenile literature. | Poisonous spiders--Juvenile literature. | Poisonous spiders--Venom--Juvenile literature. | Bites and stings--Juvenile literature.
Classification: DDC 591.69--dc23

Table of Contents

Black Widow Spider

The black widow spider lives all over the world. It is mainly found in warm places.

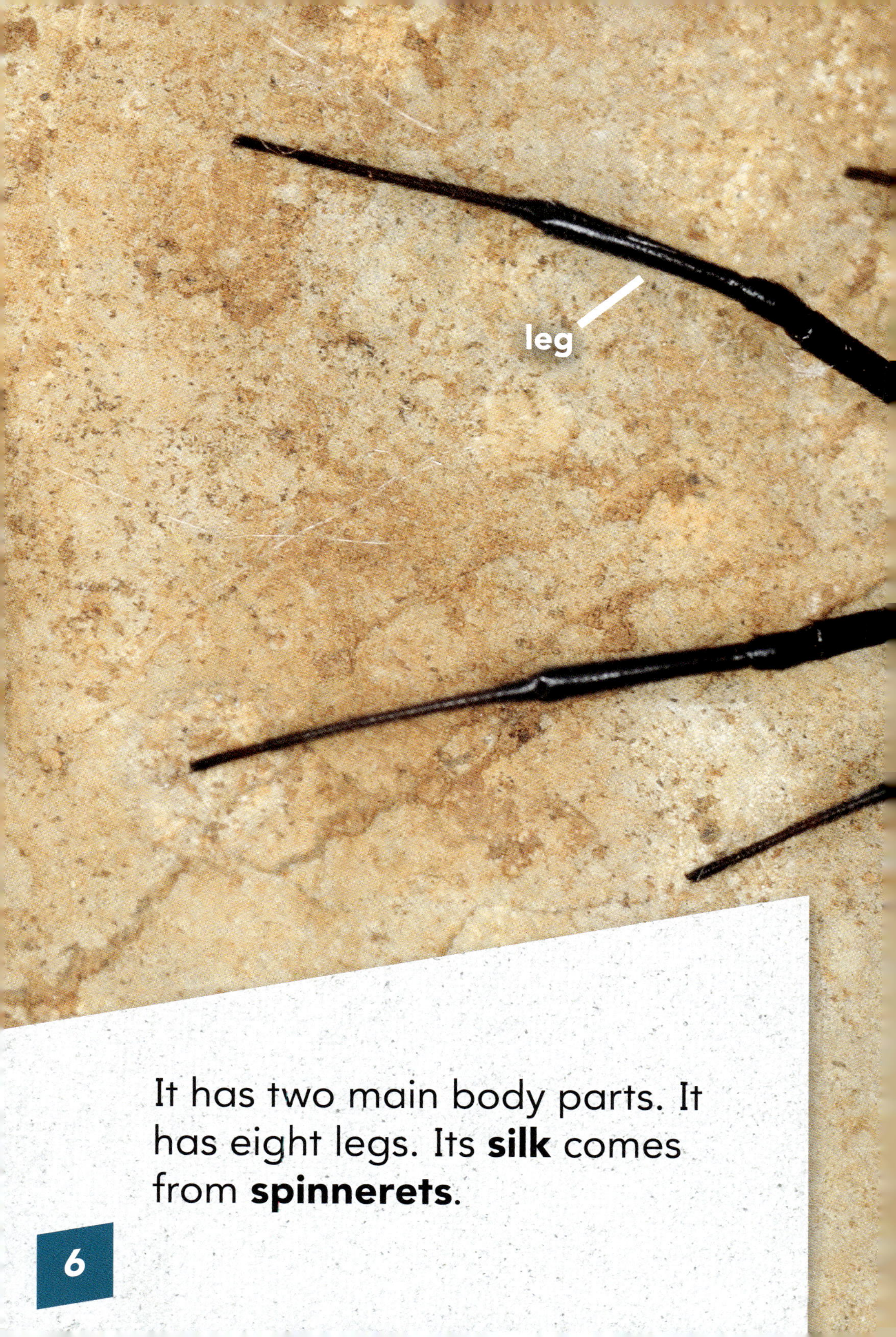

It has two main body parts. It has eight legs. Its **silk** comes from **spinnerets**.

cephalothorax
abdomen
spinnerets

Female black widows are shiny black in color. They have red markings on their abdomens.

abdomen

Males are smaller than the females. They often have brown, red, and white markings.

male

Female black widow spiders sometimes eat the males. This is how they got their name.

A black widow spider has deadly **venom**. It uses it to kill its **prey**.

A black widow spins a **silky** web. The web is sticky. It catches **prey**.

The black widow wraps its **prey** in **silk**. Then it **injects** its **venom**. It can then suck the juices out of its prey!

A black widow spider eats all kinds of insects, like flies, bees, and wasps.

More Facts

- Five different **species** of black widow spiders can be found in the US.
- Female black widows lay around 200 eggs at a time.
- A black widow spider's **venom** is 15 times stronger than a rattlesnake's! The bite is dangerous to humans.

Glossary

inject – to put into with force through a stinger or fangs.

prey – an animal hunted and eaten by another animal for food.

silk – a fine, soft, shiny fiber made by certain insects and spiders.

species – a group of living things that have similar characteristics and share a common name.

spinneret – an organ in spiders that produces the silky thread for webs.

venom – the poison that certain animals make.

Index

Online Resources

To learn more about black widow spiders, please visit **abdobooklinks.com** or scan this QR code. These links are routinely monitored and updated to provide the most current information available.